Joseph
Martinez

Copyright © 1999 by Universal Studios Publishing Rights,
a division of Universal Studios Licensing, Inc.
The Land Before Time and related characters are trademarks and
copyrights of Universal Studios, Inc. & U-Drive Productions, Inc.
All rights reserved under International and Pan-American Copyright Conventions.
Published in the United States by Random House, Inc., New York, and
simultaneously in Canada by Random House of Canada Limited, Toronto.

www.randomhouse.com/kids
www.universalstudios.com

Library of Congress Cataloging-in-Publication Data
Goode, Molly.   The land before time /
adapted for beginning readers by Molly Goode ; from a story by Judy Freudberg & Tony Geiss ;
screenplay by Stu Krieger ; illustrated by Beverly Lazor-Bahr.
    p.   cm. — "Beginner books."
SUMMARY: Before she dies, Littlefoot's mother tells the young dinosaur to go to The Great Valley,
where food is plentiful and he can start life anew.
ISBN 0-375-80160-X (trade) — ISBN 0-375-90160-4 (lib. bdg.)
I. Freudberg, Judy.   II. Geiss, Tony.   III. Lazor-Bahr, Beverly, ill.
IV. Land before time (Motion picture). V. Title.   PZ8.3.G6223   Lan 1999   [E]   dc21

Printed in the United States of America 10 9 8 7

BEGINNER BOOKS and colophon are registered trademarks of Random House, Inc.
RANDOM HOUSE and colophon are registered trademarks of Random House, Inc.

THE LAND BEFORE TIME™

ADAPTED FOR BEGINNING READERS

By Molly Goode

From a story by
Judy Freudberg and Tony Geiss

Screenplay by Stu Krieger

Illustrated by Beverly Lazor-Bahr

BEGINNER BOOKS®
A Division of Random House, Inc.

In The Land Before Time,
in an age long ago,
a dinosaur hatched...
and started to grow.

Littlefoot was the name
of this dinosaur boy.
His mom was so proud,
for he gave her great joy.

Littlefoot's mom
watched as he grew.
Grandma and Grandpa
watched over him, too.

The times, they grew hard
as food became rare.
The tree stars they fed on
no longer grew there.

Littlefoot had a tree star
that his mom had found.
He kept it for luck.
Yes, he kept it around.

Littlefoot met a friend.

Cera was her name.

They raced and they chased.

They played a good game.

This friend had three horns.

She talked very loud!

She had a hard head.

She was very proud.

One day they were
racing and chasing around
when they heard something
make a VERY BIG sound.

A Sharptooth was coming!
The noise that he made
sent both of them racing.
They were so afraid!

Littlefoot's mom ran
when she heard Cera yell.
Mom beat her long tail—
and
down
Sharptooth
fell!

The Sharptooth fell down
very hard on the ground.
And just then, the earth
made ANOTHER BIG sound!

But it wasn't the Sharptooth
that made the earth shake.
What made the earth shake
we call an earthquake.

The quake made a gap.
The gap was so wide
the moms and the dads
were all trapped on one side!

"Go to The Great Valley,
and we'll meet you there,"
the moms and dads told their kids.
"Stay together! Take care!"

But Cera told Littlefoot
in a very proud voice:
"I will go by myself!
Yes, that is my choice!"

Littlefoot did not mind.

No, he just did not care.

He just wanted his mom.

But his mom was not there!

He found her at last
where she lay on a hill.
She looked very sad
and she lay very still.

"Go to The Great Valley,
where tree stars grow thick.
I cannot go with you,
for I am too sick."

Littlefoot was so sad!

He hung his head low.

Then he met an old one,

who told him to go.

"Go to The Great Valley.

You must start today.

Your mom's in your heart.

She will show you the way."

The day he set out
was a day he was lucky.
He met a new friend,
and her name was Ducky.

Ducky could swim
and Ducky could talk.
She had a big mouth
and a very fast walk.

And what do you know?
Before the day's end,
Littlefoot and Ducky
had met a <u>new</u> friend!

His name, it was Petrie.
He did not like to fly.
But Petrie could climb
and pick tree stars up high.

Then they met Spike,
with his very slow walk.
He was strong, liked to eat,
but did not like to talk.

Then Cera showed up
and fell in with the troop.
She was safer, she knew,
if she stayed with the group.

They slept in a heap
all through the long night.
Good friends keep you warm
when the cold moon shines bright.

They took the high path
as day turned to night.
Littlefoot led the way,
for he knew he was right.

He still held the tree star
that his mom had once found.
He kept it for luck.
Yes, he kept it around.

His mom in the sky
was showing the way.
He just had to follow her,
day after day.

But Cera said, "Wait!
This cannot be the way.
I say take the low path.
The low path, I say."

The others were torn.

Take the high path—or low?

Go with Littlefoot—or Cera?

They just did not know!

Littlefoot told them, "No!

That is not the right way.

I know in my heart—

it's the high path, I say."

But they chose the low path.

They made a mistake.

The earth started rumbling.

It started to shake!

They fled to the high path.

They left Cera down there.

But proud Cera told them,

"Go ahead. I don't care."

Back on the high path,
back up on high ground,
they heard something
make a VERY BIG sound.

The Sharptooth was coming!
The noise that he made
sent all of them racing.
They were so afraid!

All were scared, except Littlefoot,
who started to plot.
Would this big bully beat them?
Oh, no, he would not!

Sharptooth could not swim,
and Littlefoot knew
if he fell in deep water,
the bully was through.

He made a good plan
that the friends carried out.
Part one called for Ducky
to let out a shout.

Sharptooth heard Ducky
and got a good whiff—

and chased her right off of
a very high cliff.

Ducky fell in the water.
She fell with a splash.
The Sharptooth fell, too.
He fell with a CRASH!

Then Ducky cried out:
"Help me! Help me, quick!"
That brave little Petrie
then did a good trick.

Petrie jumped down
from that cliff very high.
Yes, Petrie was brave.
"I can fly! I can fly!"

He pecked at the Sharptooth,
and that made him sore.
And Sharptooth gave out
a VERY BIG roar.

Part two of the plan

was to push down a boulder.

Spike pushed with his head,

then he pushed with his shoulder.

They had to work fast,
this much they all knew.
If Sharptooth got Petrie,
then Petrie was through.

Both of them pushed,

but there just was no way.

Then Cera showed up.

And she helped save the day!

The three friends pushed hard.

Yes, they pushed, every one.

The boulder fell down.

And the Sharptooth was done!

They came to The Great Valley
on the very next day.
Littlefoot had been right.
He had shown them the way.

Grandma and Grandpa and
the moms and dads, too,
were in The Great Valley,
where the best tree stars grew.